Struck

Struck

Deb Loughead

Orca currents

ORCA BOOK PUBLISHERS

Library and Archives Canada Cataloguing in Publication
Loughead, Deb, 1955-
Struck / written by Deb Loughead.

(Orca currents)
ISBN 978-1-55469-212-5 (bound).--ISBN 978-1-55469-211-8 (pbk.)

I. Title. II. Series: Orca currents

PS8573.O8633S87 2009   jC813'.54   C2009-903353-4

Summary: When Claire starts to experience success she'd never dreamed
possible, she worries that a magical event is the cause.

First published in the United States, 2009
Library of Congress Control Number: 2009929367

Orca Book Publishers gratefully acknowledges the support for its publishing
programs provided by the following agencies: the Government of Canada
through the Book Publishing Industry Development Program and the
Canada Council for the Arts, and the Province of British Columbia
through the BC Arts Council and the Book Publishing Tax Credit.

Cover design by Teresa Bubela
Cover photography by Getty Images
Author photo by Steve Loughead

Orca Book Publishers
PO Box 5626, Station B
Victoria, BC Canada
V8R 6S4

Orca Book Publishers
PO Box 468
Custer, WA USA
98240-0468

www.orcabook.com
Printed and bound in Canada.
Printed on 100% PCW recycled paper.
12 11 10 09 • 4 3 2 1

For my sister, Joanne Orsini.

chapter one

It was one of those days when you don't even want to step outside—a bleak and windy Sunday in November. And of course my mom asked me to run to the store. She was craving clam chowder. *Clam chowder*, of all the stupid things! The New England kind. Not the Manhattan kind. And she wanted it, like, right away.

"There's some money in my purse, Claire. It's in the hallway on the table."

She wasn't even looking at me. She was flopped on the sofa with the clicker in her hand, flipping through the channels.

"Why can't *you* go, Mom? I'm kinda busy right now." *Why don't you get out of the house yourself for a change? You're getting so fat and lazy!* That's what I really wanted to snap back at her. But I didn't want to hurt her feelings. They'd been hurt enough lately.

"My arthritis is acting up again," she said. "My feet are killing me." This was her usual excuse. She used to cope with it and just carry on with her day—before Dad left, that is. Ever since then, she'd been housebound. And at fifteen, I didn't want a stay-at-home mom anymore. She needed to get out and get on with her life. But Dad packed her zest for life into his suitcase and took it with him. I didn't miss him at all, but she sure did.

Besides, I had better things to do that day than running errands for my mom. I had a math test to study for, and I needed to pull up my lousy marks. I also wanted to memorize a dramatic monologue for an audition at school. Oh, and there was daydreaming about Eric. That was always a priority. He was stuck in my head like a burr on your sleeve. There was nothing I could do to shake him off.

The only problem was, I didn't stand a chance. Eric was going out with my number one rival, Lucy. She was one of the most popular girls at school—one of those girls that you never feel cool enough to be friends with. Lucy wins at everything by hardly even trying, and she is always surrounded by a flock of friends. I'd secretly wished she would be my friend. But Lucy and I had never been close the way my best friend Seema and I were. Lucy and I talked sometimes, during drama and English class, and said "hi" in the halls, but that was about it.

Sometimes I had fantasies about putting that girl out of *my* misery. But that's all they ever were, crazy, twisted fantasies. Like, what if she walked a little too close to the edge of the stage one day and "accidentally" fell off and broke her ankle? I'd have to take over her role in a play—and I would totally rock the part. I wished I could control my vivid imagination, but it just wasn't happening.

I left for the store just as the first fat raindrops started to pelt my head. A mushy mixture of rain and snow, they felt like icy needles on my scalp. I hurried along the sidewalk, thinking about my mom the entire time. I thought about the way she didn't care about herself and about her lack of interest in *anything* these days. She'd turned into a boring lump. I would never let my life turn out like hers. I would never be like her.

Dad had ditched us a few months earlier because of what he called a "midlife crisis." Mom seemed to be curling into herself like a snail into its shell. She hardly ever showered, she hardly ever moved. I didn't miss Dad's lousy moods or his hair-trigger temper. Or the way he used to grab Mom by the arm and squeeze until he left a bruise. I sure couldn't figure out why she missed it.

Her face was always a blank mask, her eyes dull and staring. She was always sighing. Oh, and asking me to run to the store to pick up random stuff that she had a craving for. Sometimes it was weird, like a jar of pickled herring, or a box of instant mashed potatoes. I'd have to drop everything I was doing and run to the store. Just like today.

Why, I wanted to ask her, *does your suffering have to interfere so much with my life? Why can't I talk to you about some of the things that are bugging me so much these days? Why is it always about YOU?* But these days mouthing off didn't even make her flinch, she was in such a sad headspace.

My life was in need of a major overhaul too. But I had no idea how I could possibly change it. There's not much you can do if you suck at math. I could study harder, maybe, but that had never worked for me in the past. And how do you "get the guy" when there's so much competition out there. It was the same thing with that coveted role in the play, the one I was going to audition for. I knew I didn't stand a chance.

The clouds were low now and purple as a bruise. Shivering, I began to run toward the main street. As the slushy rain spattered my face, curse words spilled from my lips for forgetting my umbrella. I stopped on the corner and waited for a break in traffic before stepping off the curb. For an instant I imagined how guilty my mom would feel if I got struck by a car while I was on an errand for one of her dumb cravings.

When I reached the plaza a few minutes later, I spotted it right away, stuffed into a trash can outside the supermarket doors. Thinking back, maybe I should have just run right past it.

I stopped to check it out. It was an umbrella in gorgeous rainbow shades, like stained glass or a kaleidoscope. Someone had left it there in the can. *Broken,* I thought. I spun a glance around to see if anyone was watching, then yanked it out by the curved handle and snapped it open.

It was perfect. I closed it, tucked it under my arm and hurried into the store. When I stepped out a few minutes later, it was as if someone had opened a drain in the sky. I popped the umbrella open and started walking, dreading the sight of Mom sprawled on the sofa when I got back. Of course she would be waiting for me to deliver her food.

I spun the umbrella in my hands, dwelling on all the stuff that was bothering me. It seemed as if everything was going wrong for me. Sometimes I thought I might be turning into my mom—as if her bad luck was rubbing off on me. If only, somehow, my luck could change. That's exactly what I was thinking when it happened.

First there was a brilliant flash of what could only have been lightning. I shrieked as a sharp pins-and-needles jolt shot up my arm. I was so shocked that I dropped the umbrella. My hands were shaking, my whole body vibrating. And my heart was thumping hard. It felt almost like a brush with death!

I looked up at the sky waiting for the coming thunderclap. But it never came. I frowned as I wiped the raindrops from my face.

Cripes, that was close! I thought, picking up the umbrella. *And too weird! Must be climate change messing things up.* The curved handle felt warm for some reason. I shook out my arm trying to shake off the odd tingly sensation I'd been left with. I took a couple of deep breaths and the trembling subsided. Then I looked around.

Everything else was just carrying on as if nothing had happened. Cars kept right on swishing past on the rainy street. People hurried along the sidewalks, hunched against the lousy weather, rushing to get out of the rain. Nobody else was staring at the sky. And nobody was staring at me either. No one had noticed the bizarre bolt that had just given me such a jolt.

Within a few minutes I pretty much forgot about it myself. My mind wandered back to Mom on the sofa and my jerk of a dad. And everything I had to get done that day. And Eric.

chapter two

When I stepped inside, I left the umbrella in the front hallway to dry.

Mom wasn't on the sofa where I'd left her, where she'd spent so much time the last few months. I could hear the shower running, and the sound of her voice—singing. My mom was *singing* in the bathroom. I didn't hear that every day! I wandered down the hallway and stood outside the door. She shut the water off, and then I knocked.

"Be right out, Claire." In a moment she opened the bathroom door, smiling. She had a towel wrapped around her hair and looked cozy in her bathrobe. "Ah, that feels so much better."

"I'll bet," I couldn't resist saying aloud.

"Where've you been?" she said. I narrowed my eyes.

"Where you sent me an hour ago. At the store. For clam chowder. Remember?"

"I did? Hmmm. Well, I'm not really hungry right now. Have some yourself if you want, Claire. I've got other stuff to do. I've got a plan. I'm going to see if I can find myself a job."

"Huh?" was the only word I could manage.

A plan? You've got an actual plan to find a job? This I've gotta see!

"You know how I always wanted to work as an esthetician?"

How could I possibly forget? Mom loved doing manicures and pedicures and often practiced on me and my friend Seema. She gave us facials too, and neck and shoulder massages. I always figured she'd missed her calling. But whenever she mentioned it, Dad told her she'd never be good at it and asked who'd look after the cooking and cleaning if she went out to work. Once he'd shot down her dreams, she wouldn't talk about it for a while.

"Well, I'm going out right now to apply at a couple of the local salons," she said.

"You are? Mom, that's amazing. I'm so proud of you," I told her.

"Thanks, sweetie. I figure it's about time I got the heck out of here."

"That is *so* cool," I said. "But what happened? I mean, when I left for the store a while ago, you were stuck to the sofa like you never planned to get off."

"I don't know really," she said. "It just hit me all of a sudden. This voice in my head was saying: *Enough sitting around and moping. Get on with it, Anna.* I was struck with this brilliant plan, this bolt, right out of the blue." Mom headed toward her bedroom, humming.

A bolt right out of the blue? It was like what just happened to me with the umbrella.

But it couldn't be. Getting zapped by lightning couldn't possibly change your life. Could it? Quite a coincidence—a very *weird* one.

That afternoon I didn't think any more about the bizarre coincidence. I had bigger problems to focus on, like the math quiz I had to face.

I slumped into my desk chair and flipped open the math textbook. I unwrapped one of the chocolate bars I'd just bought and chomped down on it. If anything could soothe my math worries, it was a chocolate and caramel explosion in my mouth. I stared at the jumble of numbers, waiting, as usual, for my mind to go blank as soon as I tried to solve the first problem. Numbers. How I despised them!

But something was different. When I looked at the page it was as if all the pieces had suddenly fallen into place, and I got it. I actually *got* it! I shook my head, trying to figure out why it was all making sense now. *Huh?*

I sat hunched at my desk under the lamplight, scribbling answers. I raced through each problem without a hint of hesitation. I zoomed through the math unit without stopping—until the sound of Mom's voice shook me back to reality.

She was still singing. And I was getting every math question right. Before I had a chance to consider the weirdness of it all, the phone rang.

I grabbed it before my mom could.

"Hello?"

"Claire? Is that you? You sound so much like your mom now."

Great. The one and only jerk. What could he possibly want today?

"Oh. Hi, Dad. What's going on?" I said.

"Did you enjoy our nice little dinner last Thursday night?" he asked.

Our nice little dinner. Right. A greasy burger and limp fries at some lame fast-food outlet. I spent Thursdays after school at my dad's apartment. I'd sit at the kitchen table doing my homework while he watched sitcom reruns and drank a couple of beers.

We always ordered a pizza, and then he drove me home. Now he thought he was some kind of hero because we'd eaten at a restaurant for a change.

"I'll never forget it," I told him in a flat voice. I think I heard him snicker.

"So is your mom home?" he asked.

"Yeah, she's here." I said. "Why?"

"Because I want to talk to her."

"Why do you want to talk to her, Dad?"

"I don't need to explain that to you, Claire."

"Who is it, honey?" Mom was standing in my bedroom doorway. She was dressed to go out. The last thing I wanted was for Dad to say something rotten and spoil her good mood.

"It's Dad. Should I tell him you're on your way out?"

Her face sort of lit up. Bad sign. I didn't want her to get all hopeful, the way she always did after she talked to him. He was probably just going to sweet-talk her so she'd forgive him for missing another child-support payment. Then she'd crash on the sofa again when he let her down, the way he always did. He never followed through on anything.

"No, I'll talk to him," she said. I handed her the phone without saying good-bye to him. "Rick?" I heard her say as she walked toward her bedroom. "How *are* you anyway?" Her voice practically dripped honey.

I didn't want to hear the outcome of this call. So I went back to studying math. I was still getting every answer right! As much as math suddenly made sense to me, nothing else did. That lightning bolt flashed in my mind for an instant. The randomness of it. I shivered.

Extremely weird.

chapter three

Be careful what you wish for. Why did I keep hearing those words in my head?

I couldn't stop thinking about it from the instant I opened my eyes Monday morning. When I pulled a chair up to the kitchen table for breakfast, Mom's sparkling eyes and smug smile were no help. I hoped that it had nothing to do with Dad's phone call. It was true that sometimes I half wished he hadn't walked out on us, because Mom had been miserable. But she wasn't exactly a bundle of joy *before* he left either. Usually, when I weighed the possibilities, I decided that she'd most likely get over him some day.

"Why do you look so happy this morning?" I asked her as she munched on a piece of toast and scanned the newspaper. Mom rarely got out of bed before ten, and she spent most, if not all, of the day in her bathrobe. Today she was already dressed in nice clothes.

"I just feel good today, for a change. Aren't you happy *for* me, Claire? Why do you look so suspicious?" She sipped her coffee, watching me over the rim of her cup. "*I'm* happy because I'm moving forward, going out to a couple more salons to fill out applications. Taking the bull by the horns, taking control of my life. For once!"

"That's good, Mom." I tried to muster some enthusiasm about this new positive attitude of hers, but there was this gnawing uneasiness that I couldn't deny. Why had this all happened so suddenly, and what did it mean?

As soon as I pushed through the front doors at school, I knew something was wrong. Groups of kids were talking together in hushed tones. There was a strange buzz in the air that sent a jolt of dread right through me.

Within seconds my best friend Seema was in my face, her dark eyes wide and worried. "Did you hear what happened, Claire?" she said.

I was afraid to ask, afraid to hear what she might be about to tell me, but I said it anyway. "What do you mean, Seema?"

"To Lucy. Yesterday during that freak snow- and rainstorm."

Uh-oh. Now I *really* didn't want to know. I wanted to spin around and bolt straight out the door.

"I was out in it for a while too. It was nasty," I said. "So...something happened to Lucy?"

"Yeah. She slipped on the porch steps at her house. Fell and struck her head on the concrete. She's still in hospital. In a coma."

My stomach flipped. I'd been thinking about Lucy yesterday. And not in a good way, either. Just before I got struck. *Gulp.* But it couldn't be. Could it?

"Like what...what time?"

"What *time*?" Seema stared at me as if I'd sprouted a third eye. "What does *that* matter? It was midafternoon, I think. You know, during the storm. What were you doing out in that lousy weather, Claire? Claire?"

But by then I was already walking away. I was floating through the hallway toward my homeroom in a trance. I tried to snap together all the pieces of this puzzle that my life had suddenly become. My thoughts kept spinning back in time to that moment everything had veered in a totally new direction.

And to that umbrella, now leaning in the corner by the front door at home.

I aced the math quiz in first period. Every answer leaped into my mind. It was as though my hand couldn't keep up with the speed of my brain. I finished before everyone else, and Mr. Sims sat there staring at me and shaking his head. I could almost read his thoughts. *Poor girl. She's given up already.* Boy, was he in for a shock!

"Well, that wasn't so bad, was it?" Seema said to me on the way to second period.

She nudged me and laughed the way she always did, knowing how stunned I was with numbers.

Sucking at math isn't exactly a joke, but if I didn't laugh about it, I'd cry. Once when Seema got eighty-five percent on a math quiz, she cracked up when I told her that I got the other fifteen percent. Sometimes she tried to tutor me, but she always grew so impatient when I just sat there shaking my head and shrugging. And if I ever offered an answer, she'd heave a huge sigh because it was *always* wrong.

"How do you think you did this time, Claire?" Seema was still laughing when I swiveled my head in her direction.

"You know what? I'm pretty sure I aced it this time, Seem."

"You're hilarious." She stopped in the hallway and shook her mane of raven hair. "You crack me up, Claire. Really."

"No. I'm serious. I'm pretty sure I passed this time."

Seema stared at me with surprise in her huge eyes.

"You couldn't have. You didn't have a clue how to work out those formulas last week." She frowned. "How'd you do it? Cheat notes? Let's see your hands."

I held up both palms. "How could that possibly help me, Seema? I'm telling you, it just clicked when I was studying last night. For some reason I got it."

Seema grinned. "Cool. I told you that if you worked hard enough you'd get it eventually. I'm proud of you, Claire. I can't wait to see your mark."

"Me neither," I said.

And I wasn't sure why a little shiver ran through me right after I said it.

chapter four

All through drama class I couldn't
concentrate. It wasn't because I was
thinking about what had happened to Lucy
though—or how her accident seemed linked
to my umbrella episode. No, it was because
of Eric, Lucy's so-called boyfriend.

His smoky eyes were locked on me
through the entire period. I couldn't help
staring back. And I couldn't help thinking
that if Lucy wasn't in the hospital in a coma,

this wouldn't be happening. I did my best to erase those scary thoughts from my brain.

Toward the end of class the teacher asked us all to take a seat on the stage, and Eric scrambled to sit beside me. It was a move so obvious that everyone noticed. He sat close to me, his warm arm pressing against mine. My heart was beating so hard that I couldn't pay attention. Then just before the bell, his lips were close to my ear.

"I think I've suddenly been love struck," he murmured.

Huh? "What did you just say?" I whispered back. I hoped I hadn't heard right.

"Love struck." He said it again. And my stomach did a flip.

"Uh, I think you're making a mistake, Eric," I told him. "Pay attention to the teacher, okay?" But he didn't. I could feel him staring at me the whole time.

When the bell rang I jumped, and he squeezed my shoulder and laughed. For some strange reason, that squeeze made my stomach lurch.

"What are you so nervous about today? And no, I'm not making a mistake. Have lunch with me, Claire. Okay?"

When I hopped off the stage and started walking toward the auditorium doors behind everyone else, he was right beside me. I stopped in the aisle and stared at him.

"But...but what about Lucy? I thought you two were an item."

"Oh yeah, did you hear about her?" he said. "It's nasty, isn't it? That fall she had. I feel so sorry for her family. They must be going crazy worrying about her."

"Yeah, they must be," I told him.

"But we're not really an *item*. I mean, I like her and all that. But there's just something about you, Claire. I've been noticing you more lately."

"You have?" I still wasn't sure I was hearing right.

"Yeah, I guess I really didn't know you so well before. And I think you're a good actor too. Pretty natural compared to some of the others."

"I am?" I was still trying to get the hang of this acting business. I was nervous in front of the rest of the class too, especially during improv sessions. "Well, thanks, Eric. That's nice to know." I smiled at him. I could feel myself starting to melt.

"So can I meet you at your locker at lunchtime?" he asked.

"I...guess so," I said, shrugging. What harm could it do?

"Cool." He grinned at me. I couldn't resist that grin of his. "See ya at eleven forty-five then. We can go across to the plaza and grab a slice of pizza. My treat."

"Excellent. I didn't bring a lunch today," I said "See ya then."

I stood in the hallway, watching him walk away. Then someone poked me hard from behind, and I spun around. Seema and Alice were standing there. Alice had a strange look on her face that made me squirm.

"You sure don't waste any time, do you?" Alice was frowning, and her blue eyes looked icy cold.

"What? What do you mean?" I asked.

"*Moving in* is what I mean." Her narrowed eyes were shooting poison darts.

I looked at Seema. Her dark eyes were wide. She shrugged and shook her head. I knew that Alice and Lucy were close friends, and I dreaded what I might hear next.

"Did you *wish* this accident on her or what?" Alice's voice was so cold now that a shiver ran right through me.

"What are you *talking* about?" I asked. "What is she talking about, Seema?"

Seema shrugged helplessly again.

"But *he's* the one who came over to *me*," I said. "And besides, it doesn't mean anything. I'm just having lunch with him, that's all." Why did I feel the need to explain this to Alice?

"You're having *lunch* with him? I can't believe this!" said Alice. "Do you realize that Eric hasn't even called Lucy's house to find out how she is? And now you're having lunch with him. What's *wrong* with that guy? What's wrong with *both* of you?"

Alice spun around and walked away, and left me standing there with Seema.

"What's her *problem*?" I said. "It's not like we're going out or anything."

"I don't know. I guess Alice just thinks it's kind of insensitive." Seema nibbled her thumb like she always did when she was nervous.

"Do *you* think it is?" I asked.

"I'm not sure," she said. "It's just so awful, what happened to Lucy. I can't even think of anything else right now. Only about her lying there in that hospital bed in a coma. How does this happen to someone so randomly?"

Random? Was it? *Be careful what you wish for.* An uneasiness twisted my gut, and I almost felt like barfing. How could I possibly have lunch with Eric when everyone thought that I was taking advantage of Lucy's misfortune?

The second bell rang, and I jumped again.

"Got to get to my next class, Claire. See ya later, I guess." Just before Seema made a dash down the hallway, she gave me a weird look. That look told me she didn't think going out with Eric was a good idea either, because of Lucy's bad luck or something.

Bad luck. Hmmm. Bad luck for Lucy, but good luck for me? That flash of lightning did a rerun in my brain. Again I felt the sudden jolt. The coincidences were starting to scare me. That moment everything began to change in my life. But I still wasn't sure if it was a change for the better or a change for the worse.

And that was when I made up my mind. I couldn't go through with this. I couldn't have lunch at the plaza with Eric. What would everyone think of me? They'd think I was a horrible person, that's what. I never liked to make waves. I always tried my hardest to get people to like me, not hate me.

And I didn't dislike Lucy *that* much. Sometimes I just had the feeling that she didn't like me. I couldn't help it if I had a secret crush on Eric either. And that's all it was, really. I'd never want anything bad to happen to her—it was all just a figment of my crazy imagination. Wasn't it? It wasn't possible to actually *will* something to happen, was it? And that *umbrella*! I was so confused I wanted to scream.

The rest of the morning was a complete blur. But at least I had a plan. I was going to make a run for it as soon as the lunch bell rang. I had to get away for a while, to distance myself from the school and every strange thing that had happened that day.

chapter five

I did it. As soon as the bell rang, I raced to my locker before Eric showed up, grabbed my coat and bolted for home. Only to be faced with yet another shock.

My dad's car was in the driveway. What was he doing here at this time of day? What was he doing here *period*? These days Dad avoided our house as if Mom and I were under quarantine or something. I was almost afraid to step through the door. And for good reason, it turned out.

My mom and dad were snuggled up on the sofa in the living room. They both had soft lovesick faces, and my dad's hand was on her thigh.

"What are you doing home in the middle of the day?" Mom said.

I didn't even respond. I just stood there staring at Dad. The old pain began welling up inside of me, the toxic memories of how he'd treated my mother not so long ago. It was like picking at a scab that was just starting to heal.

"What are *you* doing here? And why are you two doing *that*?" I said. I didn't try to hide the disgust in my voice.

"I used to live here, remember, Claire?" Dad's smile was sickly sweet.

"Well not anymore," I reminded him. "You chose to leave us for some blond bimbo, remember?"

"That's unfair, Claire. I met Jill *after* your mom and I split up. She wasn't the cause of our separation at all." He looked stung, like I'd just slapped him.

Yeah right, like I believe that one! "Well, we don't want you back."

"Speak for yourself, Claire," Mom said, clinging to him.

I wanted to shake her, to remind her about her new lease on life. Yesterday she was going to take the bull by the horns.

"Ouch," Dad said. "That hurts, Claire. And besides, I've had a change of heart. It struck me like a bolt out of the blue. All I've ever needed is right here in this house. So I'm back. Suck it up."

Not that bolt thing again! It was haunting me like a bad dream. My mom was wearing an expression like a contented cat. I could practically hear her purring.

"But, Mom, what about all the plans you had? What about everything that you told me yesterday? 'Enough sitting around here and moping' is how you put it. When I left for school this morning, you were about to go job hunting."

"But then Dad showed up. Just as I was about to walk out the door. It's going to be all better again, right, Rick?"

"You betcha, baby." Dad planted a wet mushy kiss on her lips. I wanted to barf.

"But why aren't you at work?" I asked him. I needed to know more. Why had he come back—what was the real story? "What happened *this* time, Dad?" But I knew exactly what I was about to hear.

"Well, I kind of got let go from my job."

His eyes were downcast now. He couldn't even look at me. I knew why. This had happened before, usually because of his slack attitude, his showing up late half the time. He was like a teen who had never grown up. He liked to play cards and drink with his buddies in the evening, go to bed late. Get up late. He was always one of "the boys," playing hockey and touch football whenever he could, just "hangin' out," as he put it. So he just kept getting "let go" and collecting employment insurance until he found a new job.

We'd always lived in a rented townhouse, and Mom's dream of owning her own home had never come true. I was sick of us living on social assistance, and I knew she was too.

But this morning I'd thought that maybe she was about to break the sad cycle.

"Let go, huh? Did you get laid off or *fired*, Dad?" I said.

"Don't be mean, Claire," Mom said. She wouldn't look at me either. She knew I wasn't happy about this turn of events.

By then my mouth felt like sawdust. I couldn't even swallow. He *couldn't* come back. Not when Mom was still trying to recover from the trauma of losing him. She'd just gotten up from spending months sprawled on the sofa. There was no doubt that if she took him back, he'd just keep doing the same thing to her over and over again, the way he always had.

I stumbled past them, my eyes a misty blur of tears as I headed upstairs to my bedroom. I slammed the door behind me and flopped onto the bed, trying to figure out why this was all happening and how I could make it stop.

I wasn't able to return to school that day. It was as if I'd been overcome with a weariness that made me do nothing but sleep. And so I slept during my parents' make-out session on the sofa and their dinner preparations. I awoke in the smudgy evening light to the sound of their gross love-laughter drifting up from the kitchen like a bad smell. There were murmurs and giggles and long pauses that had to be disgusting smooches. After sitting through a meatloaf dinner where they fed each other mashed potatoes from their forks, I felt like throwing up again. As soon as I was finished, I went to hide out in my bedroom. I looked up the word *coincidence* on the Internet.

Coincidence: a sequence of events that although accidental seems to have been planned or arranged.

I couldn't have described it any better myself, this bizarre twist that my life had taken since I had pulled that lousy umbrella out of the trash can. Ever since lightning struck, all my secret wishes, even the ones I knew were completely wrong, had actually started to come true. There was no denying it now.

And I hadn't a clue how I could possibly get my old life back. The dull one I'd been complaining about less than twenty-four hours ago. When my life seemed so complicated, it was really nothing more than normal.

I was so confused about everything that had happened that day I decided to give Seema a call. It always helped to talk to her when something was bugging me. She knew my life story inside out. Best friends forever, that was Seema and me.

"He's back," I said when I heard her voice on the phone.

"Who's back?" she said, laughing. "Give me a clue here, Claire."

"Take a wild guess, Seem."

I heard a gasp. "No! Not your dad? Why would *he* come back? I thought you and your mom were rid of him for good?"

"Apparently not. He showed up today. And Mom's actually happy about it!"

"Oh god, I'm so sorry, Claire. That totally stinks." Seema paused for a second.

"You're having a nasty day today, aren't you? First Alice, and now your dad."

"You're telling me," I said. "I'm glad it's nearly bedtime!"

Seema laughed. Just talking to her made me feel a little better. There's nothing like a good friend to dump on when your life is a tangled mess.

chapter six

Somehow, during all the confusion, I managed to piece together and memorize a dramatic monologue. I thought the monologue I created was quite clever. It wasn't very long, just some of Ophelia's crazy ramblings in act 4, scene 5, of *Hamlet*, one of my favorite scenes. And I learned it all in time for Thursday's audition.

A few weeks back, when I'd first heard that the drama club was producing *Hamlet*, I was desperate to try out for the part of

Ophelia. But as the audition date got closer, I changed my mind. There was just way too much competition, especially from Lucy, the drama queen. So I had finally decided I should just settle on auditioning for the role of Queen Gertrude, or maybe one of the male roles.

But now that Lucy was out of the picture, I figured I might actually stand a chance at snagging the Ophelia role. So that week before the audition, I chose the scene and learned my speech. Leaving out Laertes's lines made a great monologue full of drama and madness. Sort of like my life right now.

There's rosemary, that's for remembrance. Pray you, love, remember. And there is pansies, that's for thoughts...

And speaking of thoughts, I couldn't get thoughts of that moment out of my mind. I kept having flashbacks of the zap. I kept wondering if there really had been lightning, or if I'd just imagined it. Had the umbrella been struck at all? And if so, was that the trigger for all that was happening now? Was that actually *possible*? The more

I thought about it, the more I believed it. The past couple of days proved it even more. Everything really *was* different since "it" happened. And *not* in a good way.

Lucy wasn't improving at all. There were rumors that she might not make it, and that if she did, she'd never be the same. Every time I heard the buzz about it—things like "life support" and "pulling the plug" and "organ donation"—my stomach twisted and heaved.

Dad wouldn't go away either. He was slowly sneaking back into our lives, bringing more of his junk to the house every time he showed up. His mess spread into every room except mine. He even spent the night a couple of times that week. The two of them were snuggled up together under the covers again just like old times.

The peace I'd been getting used to was gone now. He always raised his voice for no reason. It reminded me how much better our lives had been without him messing everything up with his nasty attitude. I dreaded the breakup that was sure to come.

And the pain my mom would have to relive.

Be careful what you wish for, indeed...

On Thursday after school, everybody who was trying out for a part in the play got to sit in the audience and watch their rivals perform. Friends came along, too, to cheer the actors on.

My audition for Ophelia was the last one of three. Madeline and Taylor were ahead of me. They were both pretty good actors. I had my fingers crossed that my audition would be better than theirs. And as excited as I was, it was hard to ignore the feeling of guilt that kept poking at me like a knobby elbow.

I knew perfectly well that Ophelia was the role Lucy was planning to try out for. But she wasn't here. She was lying in a hospital bed across town, hooked up to all sorts of beeping machines. I could hear the whispers all around me from the other actors. Everyone was certain that if Lucy were here, she would ace the audition. And she would totally get the part of Ophelia too. Alice's voice was the loudest, of course. I was positive that she wanted me to hear her too.

"Poor Lucy," Alice practically yelled. "Too bad she couldn't be here today. She would have done an amazing job! I helped her to rehearse. Before her accident." When I glanced over, she was leering at me. I quickly looked away.

Madeline did a great job. And wouldn't you know it, she used the exact same speech as I did for her audition. Everyone clapped when she was finished too. Argh! I guess I wasn't so clever after all.

When Taylor's turn came, she tripped over her words a few times. Alice laughed and whispered to the kids she was sitting with every time Taylor blew a line. And my turn was coming up next. *Gulp.*

Sitting there beside Seema, who'd come along to watch, my stomach churned. I felt a wave of heat spreading from head to toe, like I'd stepped into a sauna. I wasn't sure if it was nerves or guilt. Why did I feel guilty anyway? The fact that Lucy wasn't here had absolutely no connection to me at all. Did it? I felt like everyone's eyes were on me the whole time I was sitting there. But whenever I turned my head to check, it wasn't true. Nobody was looking at me. I was paranoid just the same.

And that's why I bolted—just before they called my name to try out for the part of Ophelia. Because I couldn't do it. I just couldn't try out for the part that Lucy deserved to get. It didn't feel right.

I stood in the hallway alone for a while, trying to catch my breath. I wondered if I was totally losing my mind. I closed my eyes and leaned my cheek against the cool wall outside the auditorium. I breathed deeply. I sighed. I tried to muster up the guts to walk back inside and wait for my turn. Then I decided that I might as well try out for the role of Queen Gertrude or even Rosencrantz or Guildenstern instead. Eyes squeezed shut, I tried to get into character and focus on my lines. I ran through them quickly in my head. Then I heard someone sidle up beside me.

When I opened my eyes, Eric was standing there. He had his own cheek pressed against the wall. He was staring at me. He had a smug grin on his face.

"Can I kiss you?" he said.

"*What?*" My heart fluttered like a dizzy moth.

"You heard me. Let me kiss you, Claire. Like right now. I've been wanting to since we talked the other day."

"Shut *up*. You have *not*," I said. "You lie, Eric."

Why did I say that? Hadn't I been dreaming about this moment since the start of school this year? *What is wrong with you, Claire?* This was the guy who made my limbs turn to jelly. The guy I had sweet fantasies about. But for some reason, even though my whole body was saying YES to his odd request, an unfamiliar voice in my head was screaming NO!

"Uh, I don't think so," I said, backing away. "I've got to get back inside for the auditions. Aren't you trying out for a part in this play?"

"Nah," he said. "I hate Shakespeare. Let me kiss you, Claire. Come on."

Why were the hallways so empty? Where *was* everybody? Usually the halls were busy as an anthill after school. So many kids were around for clubs and sports teams. But not right now, when Eric was acting all sketchy and freaking me out. And—I couldn't believe I was even thinking it—reminding me of my *dad*! Ugh!

"Um, look, Eric, I've gotta go. Like right now."

Then he grabbed me by the shoulders and planted a wet mushy one right on my lips. There was way too much tongue involved. And for some wild reason, all I could think of at that moment, the one I'd been dreaming about for so long, was my mom and dad making out on the sofa! Gross!

I shoved him away from me. "*Stop* it, will you! *What* are you *doing*?"

"Kissing you, Claire. I know you want me to," he said.

"Oh *god*! That wasn't a kiss, Eric. That was a wet suction cup on my face! And it was totally gross! What is the *matter* with you?" He reached out and tried to hug me as I slipped away. I couldn't believe it! I gave him another shove, just to make it perfectly clear.

Then I spun around, flung open the auditorium door and stepped inside. I wished Eric's sloppy tongue would get caught in the door as I yanked it shut behind me.

"Claire? Claire Watkins?" the drama teacher called. "On stage right now, please. Your turn to audition for Ophelia."

"I changed my mind, Miss Wilding," I called out as I hurried into the darkness. "I want to try out for Queen Gertrude instead."

Yikes!

chapter seven

I had to use my Ophelia monologue when I tried out for the part of Gertrude because that was the only part I knew. I put as much emotion into it as I could. It wasn't too tough at that point. Eric's weirdness had totally creeped me out, and I was starting to think I was going crazy myself. Ophelia's mad rant wasn't much of a stretch.

I even sang the parts that Ophelia sings. I just ad-libbed a twisted little tune to go along with the words, *"Hey non nonny,*

nonny, hey nonny." And wow. Everyone actually clapped at the end of my audition, just like they did for Madeline. It made me feel good for a change.

"Claire, that was amazing," Seema said as I slid into the seat beside her to watch the rest of the auditions. "How did you pull that off?"

"I don't know," I said, shaking my head. "It just really worked for me today."

"You're *so* getting that part. You realize that, don't you?"

"Of Queen Gertrude. That would be extremely cool."

"No. *Ophelia*. You were the best one. *Honest.*"

Gulp. "But I don't *want* that part," I hissed. "That should be Lucy's part."

"But she's not here, is she?" Seema said. "Relax, Claire. What's wrong with you? It's not *your* fault what happened to her."

Then why did I feel to blame? I glanced over at Alice. She was watching me with that "ice princess" expression again. When our eyes met, I shivered and looked away.

Alice had tried out for the part of Gertrude too, and she'd done a pretty good job. I figured she should be smiling. But right now, well, if looks could kill...

I made my decision after school. Instead of heading for home, where Mom and Dad would most likely be snuggling and smooching, or fighting, I hopped on the bus and headed for the hospital. I felt the need to see Lucy. I wanted to speak to her, even if she couldn't hear me.

Lucy and I had never been close. We were just classmates who talked sometimes. I'd only considered her a rival since I'd become fixated on Eric and on the role of Ophelia. And now I couldn't stop thinking about her lying in that hospital bed on the verge of death. Her poor family must be feeling awful. And somehow, in some warped way, I felt responsible.

That stupid, stupid umbrella. It was like a curse. The minute I'd touched it and been struck by lightning, my life, and so many others', had changed directions. I'd been trying so hard to convince myself that none of it was my fault, that the lightning hadn't triggered the changes. But it wasn't working anymore. Everything was different, some of it good and some of it bad. And every bit of it was completely confusing. I desperately wanted to at least get my *own* life back on track! No wonder somebody else had pitched that umbrella in the trash! I wondered if their life was screwed up the way mine was now.

I've never liked hospitals. The antiseptic smells, the hushed worried voices. Every corner you turn, you see somebody connected to an IV, shuffling along the hallway looking like they're on the brink of death. Everyone looks sad and defeated. Ugh. That's why it was so hard to walk through those sliding doors. That, and knowing what I had to face when I got to Lucy's room.

A total nightmare!

In the gift shop I bought a tiny stuffed teddy bear to give to Lucy. It was hand-knit by someone, from the look of it. But it was cute and not expensive. The woman at the information counter directed me to the ICU up on the third floor. ICU. *Intensive Care Unit*. Where very sick people went. To recover, or not. *Cripes!*

I crept along the hallway like I was in a funeral procession. I kept my eyes straight ahead, fearing what I might see if I looked into one of those sad rooms. At the nursing station on the third floor I could barely look the nurse in the eye when I said Lucy's name.

"Lucy. Lucy Mantella."

"Her family is with her right now, dear," the nurse said without looking up. "She's down the hall, third door on the right. Wait there until someone comes out. Only two people are allowed in the room at once. And only family right now. Are you a relative?"

"Um...yes," I lied. "I'm her...her cousin."

"Okay," she said and tilted her head toward the room.

I sort of melted into a chair in the hallway, just outside Lucy's room. The door was shut. Maybe the doctor was with her now.

Maybe a nurse was with her now. Maybe I should just make a mad dash for it before the door opened. I could leave the tiny teddy sitting on the chair and bolt like a scared rabbit. I *so* did not want to face this.

And that's when the door opened. A woman was standing there looking totally destroyed. Lucy's mother, with circles under her eyes, her dark hair tangled. She jumped a bit, like she was startled to see me out there in the hallway. I'm pretty sure that I jumped too. And in that moment I lost my chance to make a run for it.

I stood up and tried to smile. It wasn't working out very well, though, because my lips wouldn't stop trembling.

"Oh. Hello. You took me by surprise," she half whispered.

"Sorry," I said. Then I held out the teddy bear, and she took it.

"How adorable! Is...is this for Lucy?"

Like a complete fool, I stood there nodding. I couldn't even speak.

"Who *are* you, sweetie?" Mrs. Mantella said. Her voice was soft and kind.

"I'm...I'm...just a friend," I told her. "My name's Claire Watkins. We're all really worried about Lucy at school. I just had to come by to see how she is."

Mrs. Mantella's face dropped, and she gasped. For one crazy instant I thought she was angry. Then she reached out, pulled me against her chest and hugged me hard.

"You can't even imagine how much this means to me," she said near my ear.

Apparently I was the very first friend of Lucy's to make that awful trek to the hospital. And I wasn't even a *close* friend! Alice hadn't stopped by yet. She'd only called the house once. Mrs. Mantella frowned when I asked about Eric. He hadn't been there either. And, for some reason, when she told me that, I wasn't surprised at all.

"It's because they're all afraid," Mrs. Mantella explained to me. "Afraid to hear what I might say. Afraid that I might cry." Two huge teardrops trickled out when she said that. "And who wouldn't be. This is a difficult thing for anyone to face." Then she squeezed my hand.

"I just felt like I needed to be here for some reason," I whispered. *Because I feel as if it was all my fault*, a little voice in my head was whispering.

"You were very brave to come," she said. "And I'm sorry you can't go into her room right now. The doctor is with her, and they're doing some tests. The good news is that she's stabilized." She managed a weak smile. "There's a fifty percent chance that she might actually pull through after all, you know."

I heaved a huge sigh. That was the best news I'd heard in days. We both stood up, and she hugged me hard again.

"I'll tell her you came by, and I'll be sure to give her this teddy, Claire," Mrs. Mantella told me. "She'll be so happy to know that you were here today."

Then she slipped through the door back into Lucy's room.

chapter eight

Dad's car was in the driveway when I got home—of course.

I walked through the front door and right up the stairs to my room. I didn't even glance toward the sofa, where I knew they were sitting. They were probably necking. Gross. I didn't need a reminder of pushy Eric and his pushy tongue.

I was still in a daze anyway, after what happened that afternoon. I didn't even want to play Ophelia, and I hoped Seema was wrong about me getting the part. I couldn't get Lucy or her mom's sorrowful eyes out of my mind now either. I thought about the guilt I'd felt looking into those eyes after all the strange coincidences. How weird that, after all the babbling that had been going on at school, nobody had even bothered to visit Lucy. As scared as I had been to go over there myself, I felt good about cheering Mrs. Mantella up for a least a few minutes.

I was just settling at my desk to start an essay, wondering if there would be any dinner tonight, when I heard it. The front door slammed—so hard the windows in my bedroom rattled. I froze. I dreaded what I might hear next. Sounds travel easily through the thin walls of low-income housing. Then I heard it. The wrenching sound of Mom's gulping sobs.

Fury grabbed my throat. How could he do this to her again? I hurried downstairs into the gloomy living room. The lights were all off, and Mom was hunched over the arm of the sofa sobbing her heart out. I switched on a lamp.

"What did he do now, Mom?" I said.

"Nothing," she mumbled into the sofa. "Go away, Claire. I don't want to talk about it right now."

"Well, we're going to," I told her. Then I settled into the sofa beside her and started rubbing her shoulder. That was when I spotted the big red welt on her forearm. I hadn't seen one for months. Coincidence? Don't think so.

"What's this?" I said, stroking it gently with my fingertip.

"Never mind," she said and pulled her sweatshirt sleeve down to hide it.

"He did it again, didn't he, Mom?" I whispered.

"No." Long pause. "I banged it on a doorknob." Her voice was muffled, but I could tell she was lying. She could never look me in the eye when she lied about Dad.

"Mom! Why do you keep letting him *do this* to you? And why did he do it this time, anyway?"

"Because..." She sniffed hard and sat up. Her eyes were pink, her face puffy and tear-streaked. But something was different this time. She was scowling, and that was a *good* thing. "Because he wanted money to buy beer, and I told him *I don't have any.* We *need* all our money to get by, don't we? There isn't any to spare, *is there*? Then... then he asked where my purse was, and I wouldn't tell him. I hid it, Claire. I hid my purse on him."

"Mom!" I hugged her hard. "You're brilliant. You really are. You've never had the guts to do that before!"

"I'm brilliant?" She looked surprised. "Nobody has ever said that to me before."

"Why did you do it, Mom? Hide the purse, I mean. Not give him any money. How come you were so brave *this* time?"

Mom sighed. I handed her a box of tissues that was on the coffee table, and she blew her nose. Then she wiped her face on her sleeve. Her eyes stopped on the welt and she touched it.

"Because I remembered the look on your face the other day when you found him here. And I remembered all the hurt.

From before. You were right, Claire." She sighed again.

I snuggled up beside her and rested my head on her shoulder.

"Mom, you want to know something?" I said. "You absolutely rock."

I didn't want to be too hopeful. I knew he'd be back. He'd done stuff like this before and slammed out of the house in a rage. But he always came back, with flowers that he picked himself or a big rainbow lollipop, something sweet and romantic. And she always softened and forgave him. And let him stay.

And the cycle would begin all over again.

Mom and I had pasta for dinner, and then I tried to focus on an essay for the rest of the evening. But every sound made me jump. I kept getting up to look out the window whenever I heard a car door slam. And that was often, because cars are always coming and going in townhouse complexes.

I made sure the doors were locked too. I didn't want him coming back here tonight or any other night. I didn't want Mom to get all upset again. I wanted her to keep trying to make a new life for herself. She was a different person when she had hope in her eyes. It almost made me think that we could do this, could actually patch a life together after all that we'd been through. We needed a life without *him* screwing everything up all the time.

I'd barely finished writing the first paragraph when the phone rang. I grabbed it before my mom could.

"*Hello?*" My voice was still angry. I couldn't help it.

Long pause. "*Claire?*"

Oh no. "Uh...Eric?"

"Yeah," he said. "Look, what's your *problem?*"

"Huh? What do you mean?"

"Come on. Don't try to mess with my head. You *know* what I mean, Claire." His voice was low and almost threatening. "You *know* you want me."

"Are you *totally* kidding me?" Now he was starting to make me mad. How could he possibly think that I liked him?

"Why'd you ditch me in the hall today? I thought we had something going on."

"We don't have *anything* going on, Eric," I said almost with a growl. "All we did was talk the other day. Then you tried to choke me with your tongue today! And now, for some bizarre reason, you think I owe you something."

"But you were coming on to me. You were giving me the vibes."

Was I? I hadn't meant to. Or maybe I had. But at that point I really *had* thought that I liked him. And I hadn't realized what a total jerk he was. Or what a crappy kisser!

"Look, Eric. It was all a total misunderstanding. And you're the one who has the problem, by the way. Please, don't *ever* call here again, okay?"

I set the receiver down. I smiled. And I started paragraph two of my essay.

chapter nine

I couldn't believe how much my life had changed in less than a week. By Friday morning it was all I could think about on the way to school. I had a running list in my head of all the strange things that had happened since the umbrella incident.

The umbrella was leaning in the front hallway at home. I hadn't touched it since I'd come home on Sunday. I was afraid that its curved handle might still be warm. Or that it might zap me again with its weird energy. Maybe my imagination was a little too wild, but I couldn't help wondering if all this really *had* happened because of that jinxed umbrella. Would it all have happened anyway?

Why did I have to spot it sticking out of the trash last Sunday anyway? I would have been better off getting soaked and avoiding this umbrella fixation! Boy, can your head ever play games with you if you let it. And boy, was I ever letting it!

In math class that morning, Mr. Sims handed back our quizzes. I was absolutely positive that every time I looked up he was staring at me. Or not—I couldn't be sure of anything these days. He walked slowly around the classroom the way he always did, setting each quiz on each student's desk facedown. We weren't allowed to look at our marks until he handed out the last one and was sitting at his desk with his hands folded. Then he would say, "Okay, gang, let's have a look"

I stared at that piece of paper on my desk, wishing I could set it on fire with my eyes. I didn't want to see an A. But I didn't want to see an E either. I didn't even want to know how I'd done at all. It was sure to totally confuse me, and I was confused enough already. So I decided not to look. I just picked up the quiz and folded it in half twice and tucked it into the back of my binder. Then I laced my fingers together in front of me and stared straight ahead.

Mr. Sims was staring right at me.

"Aren't you going to look at your mark, Claire?" he said.

"No, I'd rather not, sir," I told him. "Not right now anyway."

Everyone around me started to snicker. I wasn't trying to be funny. I really wasn't. I was just honestly afraid to look.

"Well, I'd rather you *looked* right *now*, Claire." He said it like he meant it.

"No. I think I'll wait until I get home thanks," I told him as politely as possible. "Nothing personal, sir."

There were a few snorts of laughter around the room. Behind me, Seema was digging her finger into my back and whispering, "Claire. *Claire*, are you totally *losing it* or what?"

"I'll see you after class, Ms. Watkins," he said. "Case closed."

By the time the bell rang, my armpits were soaked. I knew I was wrong not to turn that paper over, but I was trying to avoid something, I guess. I think what I was trying to avoid was finding out for sure. I was afraid to face the happiness or the disappointment. It was sure to be one or the other. Sometimes not knowing is easier, because at least you can still *hope* for the best.

I sat there staring at the scratched surface of my desk until the last person left. And I still couldn't look up at Mr. Sims.

"Claire," he said, "bring your quiz to my desk, please."

"Okay, sir," I whispered and slid it out of my binder.

I shuffled up to his desk like I had lead weights attached to my feet. Was he going to blast me for doing so well? Would he accuse me of cheating, like Seema did?

Or had I just failed miserably, as usual?

"Now open it please," he said.

Slowly I unfolded it once. Then I unfolded it again. It was still upside down on his desk. He looked at the quiz, then looked at me. He arched his eyebrows. Then his thin lips curled up into a smile. I'm pretty sure it was the first time that Mr. Sims had ever smiled at me.

"Well, what are you waiting for?"

I turned it over and stared, blinking, at the bright red mark near the bottom of the page that he'd circled twice.

"You got a C, Claire. It's the best you've done this year. I'm delighted. I knew you could do this, you know."

I didn't know whether to laugh or cry. Okay, maybe I hadn't actually *aced* the quiz, but I hadn't flunked it either! So I hadn't turned into a math genius because of that umbrella zap after all. But I wasn't a math moron anymore either. And maybe Seema was right the other day—maybe I really *was* just starting to "get it." Something I never thought would happen in this lifetime.

"Nice job, Claire Watkins." Mr. Sims held his hand out to me, and I shook it.

I walked out of that classroom beaming for the first time ever.

Seema was waiting for me in the hallway.

"Well? What *happened* in there? What was wrong with you today?"

I held out the math quiz and flapped it in front of her face. She snatched it from my fingers and started scanning it with her math-gifted eyes.

"You got a C, huh? Well, you didn't exactly *ace* it. I mean, look, how could you have missed *this* one?" She pointed at a problem, then nudged me, and I grinned. "Stick with me, babe," she added. "And you'll be sure to reach C-plus by Christmas!"

I felt pretty good for the rest of the day. I even managed to avoid Eric and his tongue.

There was no way I wanted to give him the slightest hope that I might be interested. I didn't feel a thing for him anymore.

No dizzy moths in my belly, no jelly limbs making me weak—absolutely nothing. I was still trying to figure out what the big deal had been in the first place. I'd already made a mental note to investigate a little more next time I set my heart on someone!

After school, the roles in the *Hamlet* production were posted outside the stage doors. I wasn't in a big hurry to look myself—it was just another moment that I'd been both anticipating and dreading all week. But I didn't have to look. Alice's screeching voice echoed through the hallway and nearly pierced my eardrums.

"I can't believe that *Claire* actually got *Lucy's* part! That's not *fair.*"

I froze in my tracks. Then I spun around, dashed for the exit and burst through the front doors into the cool November afternoon.

chapter ten

I ran nearly all the way home. I slowed down when I reached the complex. I was afraid to turn the corner, afraid that I might see Dad's car in the driveway and know that Mom had fallen for his empty promises again.

And sure enough, it was there. I sighed as I shuffled toward the front door. Those lead weights were attached to my ankles again.

I could hear his voice before I opened the door. He was yelling, as usual. I peeked around the corner. In the living room,

Mom was sitting on the sofa staring at the television. A red rose was lying on the carpet in the middle of the floor.

I could hear Dad ranting upstairs, and a whole lot of crashing and bashing. Mom's face was a stern mask, hard and cold. But she smiled when she noticed me standing there watching her.

"Oh, hi, honey," she said. "I'm just watching the news."

"Uh...what's going on, Mom?" I bent over to pick up the rose. It was made of plastic.

"You can throw *that* thing in the trash," she said. "I told your dad to take his stuff and shove off. I've had enough, Claire."

"He sounds really mad," I said. Then I headed for the kitchen and dropped the rose into the trash can.

"He'll get over it," Mom called behind me. "It's time for both of us to move on."

I sat beside her on the sofa, so close that our arms were touching. Dad came clomping down the stairs, lugging a huge hockey bag bulging with his junk. He did *not* look thrilled. He dropped the bag in the hallway and stared at us.

"Well, Claire, looks like it's over for good this time. You're mother's being a complete jackass. She won't even talk to me. So tell her that this is her last chance."

"Dad says this is your last chance, Mom," I told her.

"Wish him luck for me," Mom said. "Because he's gonna need it."

"Mom says good luck, Dad."

Dad let a couple of choice curse words fly before picking up the bag again. He headed for the front door, then stopped.

"Claire, sweetie, do you have ten bucks to lend to your poor old dad?" He was wearing that sickly sweet smile that used to work so well on my mom.

"Not a chance, Dad," I told him. "I'm broke too." No way he'd be getting his paws on my hard-earned babysitting money anytime soon.

"Come on, Claire. You must have a piggy bank in the house somewhere with a few loonies and toonies in it. I'll pay you back, I promise."

A *piggy bank?* I could not believe this man. "See ya, Dad," I said. My eyes met Mom's. Hers were crinkled with the slightest trace of joy.

"What the hell is *wrong* with you two?" he yelled. "You blew it this time, you know. You totally blew it. Let's see how far you get without me!"

The front door slammed. The windows rattled. Mom and I smiled.

We splurged on a pizza to celebrate. I dug some loonies and toonies out of my so-called piggy bank for the treat. Then we snuggled up on the sofa under an afghan, rubbed each other's feet and watched an old movie. When it ended, we lit a couple of candles and talked until well past midnight. We talked about everything.

I told her all about Lucy's situation and about meeting her mom at the hospital, and Mom's eyes welled up with tears. Then

I explained how I got the part of Ophelia when I didn't even want it and how guilty I felt about that. And Mom said she didn't blame me at all, that she'd feel the same way. When I told her about Eric's gross tongue, she doubled over laughing. We both did, actually. It was *sweet*.

We finally climbed the stairs to bed in the wee hours. I was asleep as soon as my head hit the pillow. I swear I hadn't slept so well in ages.

Late the next morning the phone rang, and Mom grabbed it before I could. I hoped it wasn't Dad again, begging her to take him back. But even if it was, I knew for certain what Mom's answer would be. Mom seemed different now, more confident and willing to move on. I was totally thrilled about that.

"Claire, it's for you," she said. "It sounds like a woman."

"A woman?" A babysitting job for tonight, maybe? I'd become a popular babysitter in the townhouse complex. I loved having the spare cash.

"Hello?" Hope in my voice.

"Claire? Hi, this is Angie Mantella, Lucy's mother."

"Oh, hi, Mrs. Mantella." Dread in my voice. Why was she calling me?

"I just thought you might want to know that we took Lucy off the machines this morning." My heart lurched.

"You...you did? But why?" I asked.

"Oh...oh, honey. I'm so sorry! I didn't mean to scare you. I thought you knew what I meant! She woke up. Yesterday evening. She's going to be okay."

"She is?" My heart soared. "You mean..."

"The fifty percent chance was in our favor, Claire. She's actually sitting up. And she loves the little bear you brought to her. She thinks you were so sweet to drop by."

"She does?"

Mrs. Mantella started laughing. "Yes, bella, she really does. In fact, if she's feeling a bit better tomorrow, she might give you a call. Would that be okay?"

"Sure it would," I said. "I'd be happy to hear from her." Then I remembered the part of Ophelia, and I gulped. "Tell her to call whenever she's ready."

"I will," Lucy's mom said. "And again, thanks so much. You made my day, you know. I felt so much better after finding out that the kids at school really *were* worried about Lucy even though they hadn't contacted me. Bye for now, Claire."

"Bye, Mrs. Mantella. Glad I could help," I said.

I stood there staring at the receiver before hanging up the phone. I started to feel a little itch of doubt. Could I have been wrong about the umbrella and the lightning? Was it all *nothing* more than a coincidence after all? Had I been stressing myself out over *nothing*?

As I hung up and walked away, I felt a little itch of hope, too, for the very first time that week. Because maybe, just maybe, *nothing* was my fault at all.

chapter eleven

I was dreading that phone call from Lucy. I was trying to come up with a good excuse to leave the house so I could avoid it. I didn't tell Mom that Lucy was planning to call me, but I did tell her that she was awake and was going to be fine. Mom's eyes filled with tears all over again, and this time they actually spilled out.

"Lucy's mom must be so relieved," she said, her voice strangely hoarse. "I can't even imagine what it would be like to go through something like that."

Then she flung her arms around me and hugged me so hard that I was practically suffocating. And I hugged her back just as hard.

After lunch on Saturday we both got dressed up and did each other's faces, then headed out to apply for jobs. I figured I was getting a bit too old for babysitting, even though I loved kids. It didn't quite pay enough. I was eager to find a part-time job where I could make more than five bucks an hour. Mom applied at another salon, and we both applied at the local bakery. I also dropped off a résumé at the hardware store and the supermarket where I'd found the umbrella.

It was funny how it wasn't bugging me now. I was finally starting to let it go, the thought of being struck, and of being responsible for the way things had changed. Somehow I'd survived this crazy week. So much had happened, and I had been looking for something to blame for all the weirdness.

But now it was becoming obvious that it had all been a coincidence. The umbrella zap hadn't triggered the drastic change in my fortunes after all. It was going to happen anyway. It was such a relief to get past that week-long fixation—kind of like Mom's decision about Dad.

It was strange, though, that someone had tossed a perfectly good umbrella.

Sunday morning I started to stress out again.

Should I tell Lucy that I hadn't even tried out for the Ophelia part, but I'd gotten it anyway? Or should I just wait and let somebody else tell her? Surely she'd talk to Alice as soon as she was feeling well enough. And surely Alice and some of her other friends would drop by the hospital for a visit.

But then again, how would she feel hearing the news from someone else? Would she think that I'd been sucking up to her by dropping the bear off at the hospital?

And what about Eric? Should I mention my
brief tangle with his tongue? Or would that
turn her completely against me? And what
if Alice blabbed it to her already, told her
how cozy we were in drama class? Thank
goodness she didn't catch us kissing, or I
would have been doomed.

Sometimes I thought about stuff so
much that I drove myself half crazy!

By eleven in the morning, when she still
hadn't called, I had to get out of the house.
I was going stir crazy with all my stewing
about Lucy.

"Mom, I'm going to the store," I told her.
"Do you need anything? I'm in the mood for
some butterscotch ripple ice cream."

"Works for me," Mom said. She was
doing a pedicure on her friend Lydia. It felt
so good to hear them chattering and giggling
together. I watched them for a couple of
minutes, and I said, "Too bad you can't do
this at home instead of a salon." They both
looked at me and got these huge grins on
their faces. Then I said maybe she could
make some cute business cards with fingers

and toes on them and pass them around the complex and the neighborhood.

"I could offer discounts for everyone on a fixed income in the complex," Mom said, getting all excited. "Goodness knows, some of them could use the treat. You're brilliant, Claire!" There was a new light in her eyes now. I was so proud of her.

It was overcast that morning, thick gray clouds threatening rain or snow. It was a lot like the weather a week earlier. I grabbed the umbrella as I stepped out the door. I wasn't afraid of it anymore. In fact, it almost felt like a bonus now, especially since I'd left my pop-up umbrella in my locker at school.

I took my time. I was in no hurry to get back, that's for sure. Maybe if I was gone long enough, I'd miss Lucy's call, and she wouldn't bother to phone back.

I strolled toward the intersection across from the supermarket and passed a mother fussing with her little boy. He was clutching a red ball while she struggled to pull his mittens on.

"It's cold out today, Curtis," she told him. "You don't want chapped hands."

"No, no, Mummy. Wanna bounce! Wanna bounce!" That poor mom. She sure had her hands full! The kid was cute enough though. Sometimes I wished I had a little brother, but not too often. My life was complicated enough already.

Just as I reached the curb, the red ball bounced past me and rolled out onto the road. I tried to stop it with my foot, but it rolled right over it. A car whizzed by in a blur, followed by two more. The little boy ran out in front of me. He ran right out into the road after his ball, straight into the path of an oncoming car.

Someone screamed. A car horn blared. Car tires screeched as the car slid past. I smelled burnt rubber. At that exact moment, I reached out the umbrella and hooked the handle onto the hood of the little boy's parka. I yanked as hard as I could.

He practically flew through the air. Then he landed hard on his bottom on the curb at my feet. He started to wail.

"Oh my god, *Curtis*!" His mom gathered him in her arms, and he buried his face in her shoulder. They were both sobbing.

The driver of the car had pulled over to the side of the road by that point. The poor man could barely walk, he was so shaken up. He stumbled over to the mom and little boy, wrapped his arms around them both, and then *he* started sobbing too.

It was totally amazing.

It was as if our entire lives had been spinning toward this moment—the mom and her son, the car driver, and me, all our lives. This chance moment when a group of strangers would meet—and a tragedy would be avoided. It was almost as if it were *meant* to happen that way.

And then it struck me. Maybe *that's* why I found the umbrella. If I *hadn't* snatched it from the trash that day, what then?

I watched the three of them hugging for a second. Then I snapped open the umbrella and walked away, spinning it over my head.

chapter twelve

By the time I got out of the store with the ice cream, everyone was gone. Cars were whizzing past as if nothing had happened at all. It left me wondering if anything really had happened. The only proof was the skid marks that the sliding car had left on the road.

I stared at the spot for a second, shrugged and walked home with my umbrella in one hand and my ice cream in the other. I had been tempted to shove the umbrella into the trash can for someone else to find, but after hooking that kid by the hood, I'd changed my mind. It was a souvenir now—a reminder of life's surprises.

And wouldn't you know it, the phone was ringing as I walked through the door.

"Grab that, will you, Claire? My hands are wet," Mom yelled from the kitchen.

What could I do? I dropped the bag and umbrella and picked up the phone.

"Hello?"

"Claire?" Lucy's voice was soft. She sounded so far away.

"Is that you, Lucy?"

"It's me, Claire. Just wanted to say thanks for dropping by. And for the bear."

She sounded half asleep, and I guess she was, after spending a week in a coma. I wondered if it felt anything like waking up after a long nap.

"How are you doing?" I said.

"Oh, not bad, I guess. Got some stitches in my scalp. They're itchy." Her voice was halting, with lots of pauses. "And I'm starved. I'd love a pile of poutine. Can't have that right now though."

A girl who'd just been on the brink of death, and she was craving poutine! Wow.

"I wish I could bring you some," I said. "Um...I want to tell you something, Lucy, if you have a minute."

"It's not like I'm going anywhere soon," she said and snuffled out a laugh. How could she possibly be laughing after what she'd just been through?

"Look, I want to tell you this before someone else does. I got the part of Ophelia. I didn't want it, but I got it. I hope you're not mad at me."

"Why would I be mad at you? I can't have a big part in the play now. And who says I would have gotten that part anyway?"

"Cool!" I said. And that gave me the nerve to say the next thing. "And just in case someone mentions it, Eric was coming on to me a bit, but I totally ditched him."

"*Really?*" Another pause. "Did you kiss him, Claire?"

"What? Did I *kiss* him?" *Help?* I didn't even know what to say to her. "Uh, well, he sort of kissed me, I guess. I'm not going to lie to you, Lucy. But trust me, it wasn't my idea at all."

"So? How was it?"

"How was it? You mean...um...I can't even begin to describe it."

"Well, I sure can. Nasty, huh? At least it was for me." The she laughed again. "That guy's tongue is just way too big!"

I snorted out a laugh myself, because it really was too hilarious.

"You're right, Lucy. It was a total gross-out!"

"You know what's weird, Claire. It was practically Eric's fault, my accident. I saw him from my living-room window that day. He was running down the street in the rain."

Lucy was talking slowly, almost in a whisper, taking her time telling the story. It was as if she were making sure that I heard every word. "So I ran out to the porch in my slippers to tell him to get lost. That's when I wiped out and cracked my head on the railing before I hit the concrete."

I gasped. "No way. Because you didn't want him at your house?"

"That's right. Had enough of him. My mom heard the bang when I fell. She ran out and found me lying there, so she called nine-one-one." Then Lucy drew in a huge breath and sighed. "And guess what Mom told me today, Claire. Eric was nowhere in sight."

"He left you there? He was gone by the time she found you?"

"That's right. *G-O-N-E*."

I couldn't believe what I was hearing. Eric had abandoned Lucy. He left her lying on the porch after he saw her slip and fall. How much of a jerk could one guy possibly be? Then I thought of my dad and shuddered for a second. I'd come pretty close to making the same mistake as Lucy and my mom. Falling for a loser.

"You know what?" Lucy said after a moment. "That guy is a total fungus."

"A fungus among us," I said, trying to make her laugh again. It worked too.

"Look, I've gotta go now. They're trying to get me to eat some gross mush. They say it's cream of wheat. Looks more like cream of puke. You should drop by next week. I'll be here a few more days, and I'm getting bored already."

"I'll do my best," I told her. "Get better fast, Lucy."

"Oh, I plan to. Maybe I can at least get a part as an extra in the play. And remember, Claire, *beware the tongue*," she said and hung up. And I laughed all the way to the kitchen to tell my mom and Lydia about the call.

Lydia stayed until late afternoon. Then Mom and I decided we'd have "breakfast for supper." I fried up some bacon nice and crisp, and she scrambled eggs, and we toasted English muffins. It was so yummy.

After supper we ate huge bowls of butterscotch ice cream and watched the local news. I was hit with another surprise.

A reporter was standing in the street talking into a microphone. Behind her, cars whizzed past. I recognized the intersection right away, because in the background I saw the supermarket where I'd bought the ice cream we were eating at that very moment. The supermarket where I'd found the umbrella. One week ago.

"Who is the Umbrella Girl?" the reporter was saying. "And where did she go after saving the life of Curtis Barclay today?"

I almost knocked my teeth out with my spoon.

"Hey, wait," Mom said. "Isn't that our neighborhood?"

"Looks like it," I said through a frozen mouthful.

Then, there they were, right on the screen, Curtis and his mom and the driver of the car that had almost hit him.

chapter thirteen

I didn't dare glance at my mom. I didn't want her to see the shock on my face.

"Can you tell us why you're looking for this girl, Mrs. Barclay?" the reporter said.

"Because she saved my little boy today," Mrs. Barclay told her. "With the handle of her umbrella. She just reached out and snatched him from the street, in the nick of time." There were tears in her eyes. "And I'd like to thank her personally." Curtis tried to grab the microphone, and the reporter grinned.

"The girl deserves a civilian citation or something," the driver said. "We really would like to meet her."

"Can you describe the Umbrella Girl?" the reporter asked.

"No, that's the strange thing," Mrs. Barclay said. "All we saw was her umbrella as she was walking away. She opened it up for some reason. It was a lovely stained-glass pattern. If anyone knows this girl and her umbrella, we'd love to find her."

"So there you have it, our good-news item of the day," the reporter said. "If anyone knows who the Umbrella Girl is, please contact us at the station."

When I slowly turned my head to look at Mom, she was staring at me.

"Wait a minute," Mom said. "Isn't there an umbrella like that"—she jumped to her feet, went out into the hallway and came back with it—"right in our house?"

"Where did that come from?" I said, trying to look surprised.

"I thought maybe *you* could tell *me*, Claire. I found it the other day, leaning against the wall in the hallway. And I opened it up. It has such a lovely *stained-glass pattern*. Doesn't it?" She narrowed her eyes, and a smile bloomed on her face.

Then she snapped open the umbrella.

"Mom," I said. "Don't you know it's bad luck to open an umbrella indoors?"

"Well, not this one, apparently. Aren't you going to tell them who you are? I think they'd really like to meet you, honey."

I scooped some melted ice cream into my mouth and stared at the TV. They were interviewing a politician now, so I turned it off and stared at the blank screen.

"Claire? Don't you think you should step forward? Maybe they really need to know who saved Curtis. Wouldn't you want to know if you were his mother? And that poor man who nearly struck him? They must all still be shaking."

I sighed. I didn't want to have this discussion. I'd already made up my mind. "I'm not telling them who I am, Mom," I said.

Mom closed the umbrella and handed it to me. "Show me how you did it," she said. "How did you save that little guy?"

"I just reached out the handle, like this, snagged his parka hood and yanked."

"Good thing he was wearing a parka," Mom said. "Or there wouldn't have been anything to grab onto."

"Good thing I found the umbrella in the trash a week ago, Mom. And that I had a craving for ice cream. Otherwise...well, you know..."

It was Mom's turn to sigh. "Boy, life can be weird sometimes, can't it?"

"No kidding," I said.

"I still think you should meet with them, Claire. Don't you think they deserve to know?" Mom sat down beside me and started running her fingers through my hair, the way she used to do during our mother-daughter moments. It felt good. "I mean, they think you deserve a reward!"

"I don't need a reward for *that*," I told her. "I just did what anyone else would have done. And let them wonder who it was.

It doesn't hurt to have a bit of mystery in your life, does it? You don't always have to know how or why something happened. Sometimes you just have to smile and let it go."

Mom cupped my chin in her hands and looked me right in the eye.

"You want to know something, Claire Watkins?" she said as she pulled me against her and hugged me hard. "You absolutely rock."

"You want to know something, Anna Watkins?" I said beside her ear. "I really hope I turn out to be just like you some day."

I hugged her back, even harder than she was hugging me, that amazing mother of mine. Because I knew right then and there that she was going to be okay.

We both were.

Deb Loughead is the author of numerous poems and short stories, as well as *Chendra's Journal* and *Mystery of the Serpent Ring* (Scholastic, 2008) and *Time and Again* (Sumach, 2004). Deb lives in Toronto, Ontario.

Orca Currents

121 Express
Monique Polak

The Big Dip
Melanie Jackson

Bio-pirate
Michele Martin Bossley

Camp Wild
Pam Withers

Chat Room
Kristin Butcher

Cracked
Michele Martin Bossley

Crossbow
Dayle Campbell Gaetz

Daredevil Club
Pam Withers

Dog Walker
Karen Spafford-Fitz

Explore
Christy Goerzen

Finding Elmo
Monique Polak

Flower Power
Ann Walsh

Fraud Squad
Michele Martin Bossley

Orca Currents

Horse Power
Ann Walsh

Hypnotized
Don Trembath

In a Flash
Eric Walters

Junkyard Dog
Monique Polak

Laggan Lard Butts
Eric Walters

Manga Touch
Jacqueline Pearce

Marked
Norah McClintock

Mirror Image
K.L. Denman

Nine Doors
Vicki Grant

Pigboy
Vicki Grant

Perfect Revenge
K.L. Denman

Queen of the Toilet Bowl
Frieda Wishinsky

Rebel's Tag
K.L. Denman

Orca Currents

See No Evil
Diane Young

Sewer Rats
Sigmund Brouwer

The Shade
K.L. Denman

Skate Freak
Lesley Choyce

Special Edward
Eric Walters

Splat!
Eric Walters

Spoiled Rotten
Dayle Campbell Gaetz

Sudden Impact
Lesley Choyce

Swiped
Michele Martin Bossley

Watch Me
Norah McClintock

Wired
Sigmund Brouwer

Visit www.orcabook.com for all Orca titles.